This edition published 2006
By Zero To Ten Limited,
Part of the Evans Publishing Group,
2A Portman Mansions, Chiltern Street, London W1U 6NR

Reprinted 2009

Text copyright © Hilary Robinson 2005
Illustrations copyright © Mike Gordon 2005
Additional illustration work by Carl Gordon

British Library Cataloguing in Publication data:
Robinson, Hilary
        Croc by the rock
        1. Children's stories Pictorial works
        I. Title
        823.9'14 [J]

ISBN 9781840894578
Printed in China

Croc
by the
Rock

by Hilary Robinson
illustrated by Mike Gordon

ZERO TO TEN

When Jake took his net...

...to fish by the rock

he saw what he thought...

...was the eye of a croc!

"A croc by the rock!"
Jake called to the man...

...who let his dog out

from the back of a van.

The dog stretched his paws

then raced round
the rock...

...then jumped in the lake

to hunt for the croc!

He dipped and he dived

as the kids rushed to take...

...some photographs of

the croc in the lake.

Then everyone cheered

as the dog showed to all...

...that the crocodile's eye

was only a ball!

But later that day

Jake fished on the rock...

...and found in his net...

...a tooth from a croc!